WHEN TURTLE GREW FEATHERS

A Folktale from the Choctaw Nation

Tim Tingle

Illustrated by Stacey Schuett

AUGUST HOUSE
Little folk

ATLANTA

Published 2007 by August House LittleFolk,
Atlanta, Georgia

www.augusthouse.com

Book design by Diane Kanzler, HK Design

Printed by Pacom Korea
Seoul, South Korea

10 9 8 7 6 5 4 3   PB

LIBRARY OF CONGRESS CATALOGING-IN-PUBLICATION DATA
Tingle, Tim.
When Turtle grew feathers : a folktale from the Choctaw nation / Tim Tingle ;
illustrated by Stacey Schuett.
   p.   cm.
Includes bibliographical references.
ISBN-13: 978-0-87483-777-3 (hardcover : alk. paper)
ISBN-13: 978-1-93916-021-8 (paperback : alk. paper)

1. Choctaw Indians—Folklore. 2. Turtles—Southern States—Folklore.
3. Tales—Southern States. I. Schuett, Stacey, ill. II. Title.
E99.C8T57 2007
398.2089'97387—dc22

                                                      2006026841

*The paper used in this publication meets the minimum requirements
of the American National Standards for Information Sciences—Permanence
of Paper for Printed Library Materials, ANSI.48–1984.*

To Teagan Elise Tingle,
first granddaughter.
–TT

For Ian and Clare, who both make
surprising flights of their own.
–SS

Most everybody knows about the race between Turtle and Rabbit. But the Choctaw people tell the story differently. They say that the reason Rabbit couldn't outrun Turtle was that he wasn't racing a turtle at all. He only thought he was. It all took place on the day when Turtle grew feathers.

Turkey was walking in the grass by the lake. He was stretching his long skinny neck, not watching where his feet fell.

Turkey didn't see Turtle napping in the grass.

Currrr-rack! Currrr-rack!

"You stepped on my back!" said Turtle.
"My shell is shattered like glass!"

"I'm not to blame," said Turkey.
"You sleep too low in the grass."

"My shell is my home," said Turtle.
"You broke my beautiful shell!"

"That's your fault, not mine," said Turkey.
"I'm tired of hearing you yell."

Turkey lifted his wings to fly away.

"Wait!" cried broken-shelled Turtle.
"Let's call a truce and not fight."

Turkey smiled and nodded.
"Let's do what we know to be right."

Just then an army of ants paraded by.

"Friends," said Turkey, "help us mend this shell.
Then I'll help you gather your dinner till your
little bellies swell."

So the ants went to work. With threads of silk from
the cornfield, they sewed Turtle's shell together.

Turtle climbed into his shell. It was as good as new.

"I'm sorry for your trouble," said Turkey. "But I like your shiny shell."

"Want to try it on?" asked Turtle. "I think you would look just swell."

"I believe I would," said Turkey.

Turtle shimmied out of his shell, and Turkey climbed in. He stuck his long neck out the front. He pushed his wings through the sides. He poked his long skinny legs out the back of Turtle's shell.

About that time, five Little Bitty Turtles came huffing and puffing and running down the path.

"Everybody hide!" the Little Bitty Turtles cried.

"What is it?" asked Turtle, his eyes opened wide.

"Here comes Rabbit," said the Little Bitty Five. "Rabbit wants to race, and he won't be denied."

Turkey pulled his wings and legs into Turtle's shell.
He drew his head inside and peeked out the front.
In the flick of an eye, Rabbit burst into the clearing.

"I feel real fast! I'm ready to race. Who wants a little mud in his face?"

He spotted Turtle's shell lying on the ground.

"How about you, Turtle? How about a little race?"

Turkey lay hidden in Turtle's shell and didn't say a word. Rabbit moved closer.

"I said, how about you, Turtle? How about a little race?"

Finally, from where he hid in the grass, Turtle yelled, "Get it on!"

Rabbit jumped back. He had never been talked to like this!
He scratched a line in the dirt, puffed his chest out, and said,

"You've made me mad, my slowpoke friend.
Your racing days are about to end!"

Turkey waddled to the starting line. He seemed to take forever.

Finally, Rabbit said, "Once around the lake when I say 'Go!'
Careful not to run too slow!"

Turkey poked his head out and looked around. Rabbit had never seen a turtle like that before! While he watched, that neck kept growing, and growing, and *growing*! Rabbit was beginning to get a little worried.

"On your mark," said Rabbit.

Long, skinny legs grew out of the turtle shell.
Rabbit couldn't believe what he was seeing.

"G-g-g-g-get set," said Rabbit.

But the strangest thing was yet to come.
All of a sudden, wings popped out of the
turtle shell—long, slow-flapping wings!

Rabbit was downright scared by now.
He stuttered. He stammered. He finally
shouted,

"G-g-g-g-g-go!"

Turkey took off in an explosion of dust. His legs were churning and his wings were flapping. Rabbit stayed behind, choking in the dust. Just as he was about to take off, he heard a sound behind him.

Screech! Turkey was coming in for a landing! He had already circled the lake.

Turkey glanced over at Rabbit. He adjusted his shell till it fit properly. He dusted himself off with his feathers, then he strutted across the finish line.

Rabbit looked on, unable to speak. His eyes were as big as Little Bitty Turtle shells.

For the first time ever, Rabbit couldn't think of a thing to say. He hung his ears and went *hip-hoppity, hip-hoppity,* off to where rabbits hide.

Rabbit never challenged Turtle again. That's why you never see them racing today.

That's the way the Choctaws tell the story. It all took place, they say, on the day when Turtle grew feathers.

It was a day of great learning as well. Turtle learned you don't have to be the biggest, or the fastest, or the best. But it sure is nice to be friends with those that are!

Chata haptia hoke! Now the story is yours.

SOURCES

Bushnell, David. *Myths of the Louisiana Choctaws*. Bureau of American Ethnology, 1909.

Jones, Charley. Oral interview. August 1992.

McAlvain, Jay. Tape-recorded interview. November 1992.